# Message in the Mooncake
## A Legend from Ancient China

words by **Sapphire Chow**

art by **Xiaojie Liu**

**Barefoot Books**
step inside a story

The smells in the market tickle my nose. The sour aroma of fermentation, the sweet scent of fried dumplings, and the stink of fish stalls make me hungry and gag all at the same time.

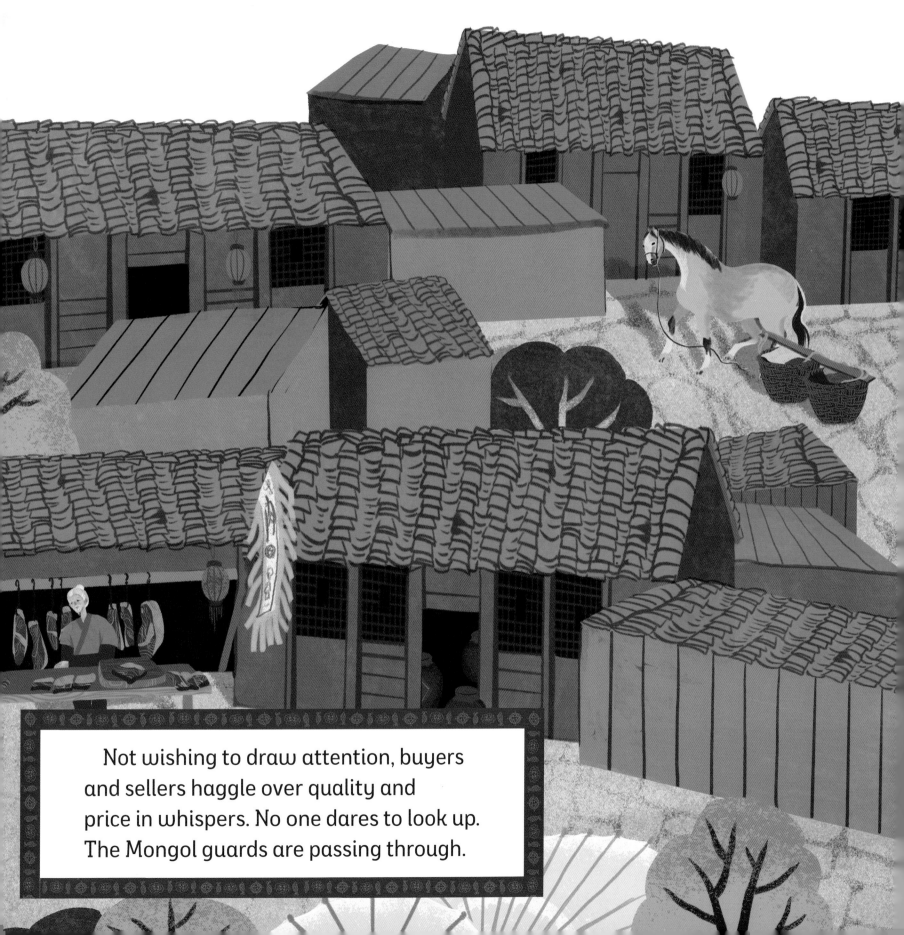

Not wishing to draw attention, buyers and sellers haggle over quality and price in whispers. No one dares to look up. The Mongol guards are passing through.

"Time to go, Su-Ling," Ma-Ma says.

I am trying out new kung fu moves.
I stop my Tiger Kick in mid-air.

We exit the market, each
with a pack on our backs.

Ma-Ma holds baby Ming and I
have the meat and vegetables.

We pass a Mongol guard. Ma-Ma shuffles by with her head down. I skip by with my head up, my unblinking eyes glaring at him.

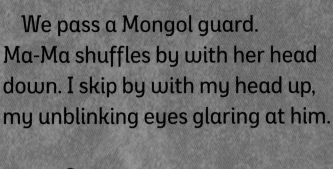

His sharp spear is scary, but his lips curl up in a grin.

Maybe he is trying to show he's friendly, but I know that the Mongols have made life very difficult for us. They have made it against the law for Chinese people to gather in groups for any reason, so that we cannot plan a rebellion.

That night, just before dinner, Pa-Pa bursts through the door with exciting news.

## "We are planning a revolt!"

Ma-Ma gasps. She shuts the windows and locks the door. "But how?"

"Soon it will be Mid-Autumn Festival," Pa-Pa says. "The pastry shops will put a message inside one of the four mooncakes in every box. It will say when to strike so we can be unified in our attack."

# THE TIGER LEAPS UP!

It's a perfect plan!

"But there is one problem," Pa-Pa continues. "The guards might stop and search people carrying the mooncakes."

"So, what do we do?" asks Ma-Ma. "We should at least deliver cakes to Uncle Ming and Pho-Pho so they are prepared for the attack."

"I can deliver the cakes," I tell Pa-Pa.

Pa-Pa pulls me close. "Su-Ling, can you deliver them without getting caught?"

I nod my head. Ma-Ma shakes hers.

"It's too dangerous," Ma-Ma cries. "She's only a girl!"

Two days later, Pa-Pa arrives home with two boxes under his jacket. We gather around the table. Pa-Pa opens a box.

Inside are four mooncakes, each with a different flower pattern — chrysanthemum, lotus, peony, and plum blossom.

Pa-Pa cuts each cake carefully. The message is in the cake with the peony flower pattern.

It says: *On the 15th day of the 8th lunar month, on the day of the full moon, commence attack at midnight.*

That is two days away. We must deliver the cakes **tonight.**

We eat dinner in silence, but my heartbeat rings in my ears. My mind whispers doubts.

"You ate so little," Pa-Pa says gently. "I'll keep the soup warm for your return."

I put on my quietest shoes and my black cloak. My hands are shaking. Pa-Pa pats me on the back. "We're counting on you."

I nod my head. Ma-Ma shakes hers. She hugs me for too long. "Be careful."

Pa-Pa packs me everything I need:

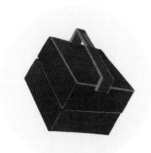

a box of mooncakes,

a candle,

green and
red lanterns,

and matches.

"If you are successful, light the green lantern for your walk home. Then the village will know that another message has been safely delivered. If the guards capture the mooncake and find out about our plan, then light the red lantern to call off the revolt."

I nod and take the lanterns. Then I slip into the night.

*Heavy footsteps!*
I duck behind a tree.

THE TIGER HIDES
IN THE SHADOWS.

I shuffle around the
tree keeping pace with
the marching guards.

Turning my head to watch the
receding figures, I sprint ahead and
immediately crash into a tall tree.

The tree speaks to me.

"Hello, kung fu kicking girl!
Where are you going this evening?"

I recognize the guard
who grinned at me in
the market. I am unable
to speak. The Mongol's lips
move but the boom-boom of
my heart prevents me from
hearing the words.

SHALL I RUN?
NO, NO, HE CAN
PROBABLY RUN FASTER.
THE TIGER IS TRAPPED.

The guard takes me to a tent, where he sits me down in front of the General. He dumps my bag onto the table. Then he pulls out a knife.

# THE TIGER FEARS FOR ITS LIFE.

"Those look good. Let me have a taste," the General says. A mooncake is cut and he eats a piece. He cuts open another.

# THE TIGER FINDS COURAGE TO SPEAK.

**These are for Pho-Pho!**

I am weeping, but I'm not sure if I am pretending.

I peek inside the box. The peony and the lotus are untouched. The knife cuts into the peony. I stop breathing. Pa-Pa, I have failed you.

"General, Sir," calls a voice. "I'm leaving to inspect a fire in the east."

The soldiers turn to the voice. I nudge the box to the edge of the table. The cake with the peony topples to the floor.

"Oh no!" I jump forward to pick it up and lightly step on the cake.

# THE TIGER IS QUICK-THINKING.

I peel the cake off the floor and scrape the sticky goo from my shoe.

I pick specks of dirt off the cake while checking that the message is still hidden.

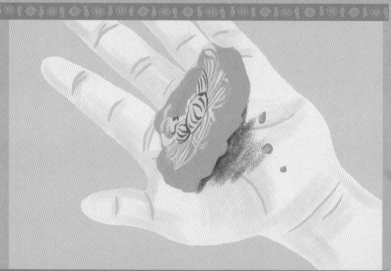

"That's enough!" yells the General.
"Pack up your things and go."

THE TIGER RUNS AND RUNS.

"Whoa, little tiger . . . slow down," says Uncle Ming. "You brought me mooncakes?"

I give the box to Uncle Ming.

Pho-Pho looks confused. "Some of these cakes look squashed or nibbled. Did you fall when you were running? Did you eat the other cakes, Su-Ling?"

Between large gulps of air, I tell them what happened. Uncle Ming pulls out the secret message. He squints his eyes but I see the twinkle. He nods and then he smiles. He goes on one knee and looks straight into my eyes.

You have been extremely brave tonight. Because of what you did, our village can join the revolt. Pho-Pho and I are very proud of you.

I feel the sting behind my eyes and throw my arms around Uncle Ming.

Pho-Pho fixes the candle into the holder on the green lantern and lights it for me. She hugs me tight.

You better hurry home. And be careful. Stay on the main streets so all our friends can see you.

Once again, I slip out into the night.
I don't see the eyes in the windows of
the houses I pass, but I know everyone
is watching. The candle in the green
lantern glows brightly.

AND AT LAST . . .

THE TIGER ROARS!

# THE YUAN DYNASTY

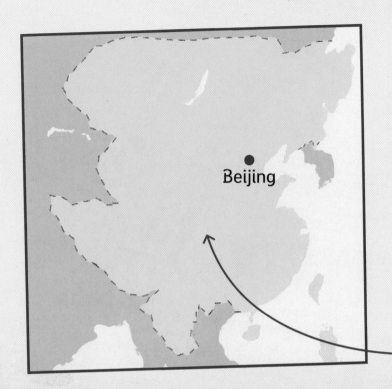

Beijing

China in the Yuan Dynasty

A dynasty is a line of rulers all from the same family. In this story, Su-Ling lives during the Yuan (*yoo-EHN*) Dynasty in ancient China, which lasted from 1271 until 1368. It began when Mongolian Emperor Khubilai Khan (*koo-buh-lai KAHN*) conquered China, and it was the first time China was ruled by a group of people who weren't Chinese.

# EVENTS IN THE YUAN DYNASTY:

**1271**
The Yuan Dynasty begins with Khubilai Khan, the fifth Mongol emperor, becoming emperor of China.

**1280s**
Paper money is invented, which makes it easier for people to buy and trade things. Coins fall out of use.

**1279**
Khubilai Khan's army conquers the Southern Song Dynasty, uniting all of China under Mongol rule.

# THE MONGOLIAN INVASION

The Mongol army was a group of fierce warriors, skilled archers, and expert horse riders. In the 1200s, led by Genghis Khan (*GENG-iss KAHN*), they embarked on the Mongolian Invasion, conquering many lands in Asia and creating a mighty empire that lasted about 100 years.

## IS MESSAGE IN THE MOONCAKE A TRUE STORY?

This is a retelling of a well-known folktale about the cleverness and bravery of the Chinese people during the Mongol occupation. All the different versions involve passing hidden messages in Mid-Autumn Festival mooncakes to organize a rebellion. The legend does not feature a child delivering the message — that element is the author's own invention. We don't know for sure if the folktale is based on true historical events or if it's simply an exciting and inspiring story.

### 1290s
The Italian explorer Marco Polo visits China and meets with Emperor Khubilai Khan.

### 1368
The Yuan Dynasty ends as the Red Turban Rebellion takes over and the Ming Dynasty begins.

# THE MID-AUTUMN FESTIVAL

The Mid-Autumn Festival takes place on the 15th day of the 8th lunar month, which usually falls in September or October, and is celebrated throughout China and other Asian countries. Families come together for a big feast and to eat mooncakes. Lanterns of all shapes and sizes light up the night and parades line the streets. The Mid-Autumn Festival is a time for joy, gratitude, and spending time with loved ones under the moonlight.

# WHAT IS KUNG FU?

Chinese martial arts is also known as kung fu. It includes several fighting styles, which have existed for centuries. Kung fu is known for trickery and quickness, but it is not just about fighting — most of all, it is about discipline, respect, and self-improvement. It takes a lot of hard work and dedication. In this story, the tiger represents the confidence, bravery, and inner strength that Su-Ling has developed through kung fu.

# MANY TYPES OF MOONCAKES

Cantonese-style

Teochew-style
(*tyoht-SHOO*)

Yunnan-style
(*YOON-nahn*)

Beijing-style

Suzhou-style
(*SOO-djoh*)

Hong Kong-style

Mooncakes are made of a dense, sweet filling (usually lotus seed paste or black sesame seed paste) wrapped in a pastry and pressed into a decorative shape before baking. Fancier cakes can have a salted egg yolk at the middle, symbolizing the full moon.

Traditionally, mooncakes were used as offerings to the moon and symbolized family unity and togetherness. They are often given as gifts between family members and friends as a way of expressing blessings for the future.

Over the years, mooncakes have evolved, and now, mooncakes can vary in taste, filling, crust, and appearance. They are usually store-bought, since they are quite complicated to make at home.

*In loving memory of Sapphire Chow, who wrote her stories
for her grandchildren, Garrett and Heather*

*To my daughter, Liuyu, a little girl born with wisdom. May you be as smart and brave as Su-Ling – X. L.*

# AUTHOR'S NOTE

What inspired me to write this book? Numerous stories surround the Mid-Autumn Festival, the most popular one being about Chang Er (also known as the Moon Goddess). Yet the story that I grew up with is the myth about distributing mooncakes with a secret message to aid the revolt against the Mongols. My research unearthed many picture books on Chang Er, but none about messages in mooncakes, and I felt this story deserved to be told.

**— Sapphire Chow**

# ILLUSTRATOR'S NOTE

As an illustrator, I am inspired by traditional Chinese culture and artwork, as well as the Fauvist painters such as Matisse. The most difficult part of making this book was depicting all the historical details of Yuan Dynasty China while also bringing Su-Ling's story to life. I celebrate the Mid-Autumn Festival every year, and I love eating mooncakes and drinking tea while spending time with my family. The kind of mooncake I love best has layers of puff pastry on the outside and a sweet, delicious filling.

**— Xiaojie Liu**

Barefoot Books is deeply grateful to the family of Sapphire Chow and to Anjanette Barr of Dunham Literary for their support and assistance in the creation of this book. We would also like to thank the following consultants:

**Emily Golightly**, Media Coordinator / Librarian, Newport Elementary School
**Dr. Melody Ann Ross**, Assistant Professor of Linguistics, University of Duisburg-Essen
**Nancy Steinhardt**, Professor of East Asian Languages and Civilizations / Curator of Chinese Art
at the Museum of Archaeology and Anthropology, University of Pennsylvania

Barefoot Books
23 Bradford Street, 2nd Floor
Concord, MA 01742

Barefoot Books
29/30 Fitzroy Square
London, W1T 6LQ

Reproduction by Bright Arts, Hong Kong. Printed in China
This book was typeset in CC Sign Language, Eixample Dip,
and Scriptorama Markdown
The illustrations were created digitally

Hardback ISBN 979-8-88859-228-1
Paperback ISBN 979-8-88859-229-8
E-book ISBN 979-8-88859-301-1

First published in the United States of America by Barefoot Books, Inc
and in Great Britain by Barefoot Books, Ltd in 2024
All rights reserved

British Cataloguing-in-Publication Data:
a catalogue record for this book is available from the British Library

Library of Congress Cataloging-in-Publication Data
is available under LCCN 2024932219

Graphic design by Lindsey Leigh, Barefoot Books
Edited and art directed by Lisa Rosinsky, Barefoot Books
Endnotes by Erin Lueck, Barefoot Books

1 3 5 7 9 8 6 4 2